The Actor, the Rebel, and the Wrinkled Queen

by Terry Deary
illustrated by Helen Flook

PICTURE WINDOW BOOKS
Minneapolis, Minnesota

Managing Editor: Catherine Neitge
Story Consultant: Terry Flaherty
Page Production: Tracy Davies
Creative Director: Keith Griffin
Editorial Director: Carol Jones

First American edition published in 2006 by
Picture Window Books
5115 Excelsior Boulevard
Suite 232
Minneapolis, MN 55416
1-877-845-8392
www.picturewindowbooks.com

First published in Great Britain by
A & C Black Publishers Limited
37 Soho Square, London W1D 3QZ
Text copyright © 2003 Terry Deary
Illustrations copyright © 2003 Helen Flook

Library of Congress Cataloging-in-Publication Data
Deary, Terry.
    The actor, the rebel, and the wrinkled queen / by Terry Deary;
illustrated by Helen Flook.
        p. cm. — (Historical tales) (Read it! chapter books)
    Summary: A young actor at the Globe Theatre must defend his master
when Queen Elizabeth suspects that Shakespeare tried to help the Earl of
Essex overthrow her.
    Includes bibliographical references.
    ISBN 1-4048-1297-0 (hardcover)
    1. Great Britain—History—Elizabeth, 1558–1603—Juvenile fiction.
2. Elizabeth, I, Queen of England 1533–1603—Juvenile fiction. 3. Essex,
Robert Devereux, Earl of, 1566–1601—Juvenile fiction. [1. Great Britain—
History—Elizabeth, 1558–1603—Fiction. 2. Elizabeth, I, Queen of England
1533–1603-Fiction. 3. Essex, Robert Devereux, Earl of, 1566–1601-Fiction.]
I. Flook, Helen, ill. II. Title. III. Series: Deary, Terry. Historical tales. IV. Series:
Read it! chapter books.
    PZ7.D3517Act 2005
    [Fic]-dc22   2005007214

Table of Contents

*This book is dedicated to the memory
of the victims of Queen Elizabeth's torturers
and executioners, whose only "crime" was to follow
the wrong religion.—Terry Deary*

The Dragon Queen

Queen Elizabeth was a monster. A monster who had hands like claws; a red, frizzy wig like a lion's mane; a wrinkled, white face, caked with a mask of makeup, like a corpse in a coffin; little, black, rotting teeth; and breath like a sick, old dog.

I met her just before she died, and she was the most scary thing I'd ever seen in my life.

Her dress was crusted with jewels and shone red, green, blue, orange, and white, like a dragon's scaly skin. Her short, fat fingers pinched my ear, and she dragged me forward so my button nose was a hand's breadth away from her little, hooked beak of a nose.

That's when I smelled her stinking breath and heard her creaking voice hiss to my face.

"The worst is death, and death will have his day," she breathed.

"Yes, your majesty," I tried to say, but my mouth was dry and I just squeaked, "Yessum-ad-stee!"

"Yessum-ad-stee?" she mocked me. "You are supposed to be an actor, boy. You are supposed to speak every word clearly, aren't you?"

"Yessum-ad-stee!"

"Does Mr. Shakespeare let you speak like that onstage?"

"No-hum-ad-stee!"

"Then do not speak like that to your queen!" she snarled.

At last she let me go and I swayed, almost fainting.

A small, round man with a white beard grasped my arm and held me up. He was Lord Cecil, the queen's chief minister.

She turned her little dark eyes on him. "Let the boy kneel ... dwarf."

Lord Cecil chewed his lip. I could tell he hated being called dwarf.

"Do you want to die?" the queen asked suddenly.

"'No!" I said and my voice was loud and clear this time. Lord Cecil gave me a small kick on the ankle.

"No ... your majesty," I said more softly, and lowered my eyes to the cold stone floor.

"Then you know what you must do?"
Lord Cecil asked in a kindly voice.

"Tell you the truth," I nodded.

"One lie and you go back to the prison
cell," Queen Elizabeth said. "Or, we may take
you along to the Tower of London to let you
try out some of our torture machines. The
rack, the red-hot pincers, the thumbscrews ..."

"I'll tell the truth!" I moaned. "I will!"

"Then let us begin," the queen commanded, and she sat back on her throne to listen.

I told my story.

The Red-haired Girl

My name is James Foxton and I come from a village near York in the north of England. When I was about five years old, a troupe of actors came to York and put on a show.

It was magical. For two hours, I forgot the misery of my empty belly and the cold that bit at my bare feet.

"I want to be an actor just like them," I told my parents.

My father laughed, but my mother said, "The boy can sing and dance well enough.

Let him join a company of actors. He'll be one less hungry mouth for us to feed. We haven't enough food as it is. The lad will only starve to death if we keep him at home."

So, at the age of seven, I joined Mr. William Shakespeare's actors at The Globe theater in London. At first, I helped with the costumes and helped the actors to dress. I made sure they had the right swords and crowns, or wigs or wine bottles, before they went on stage. Then I was given a small part as a fairy in Mr. Shakespeare's play, *A Midsummer Night's Dream.*

Of course, all the parts were played by boys and men—girls and women were not allowed to act on the stage. That's what started the argument with the blue-eyed, red-haired girl at the Black Bull Inn. We often put on a play in the yard of some inn like the Black Bull.

I played the part of a fairy called Cobweb, and at the end, the crowd cheered and clapped when I came on stage to take my bow.

The red-haired girl just glared at me from the doorway into the barroom. When I had changed out of my dress, I went into the Black Bull to eat. The girl served greasy mutton stew and spilled it on my shoulder.

"Oh, dear, what a shame!" she smirked.

I knew she had done it on purpose.

She mopped at it with a dirty rag, and I pushed her hand away.

"Ooooh! Is the little fairy girl upset?" she asked.

"Shut up," I snapped.

"Ooooh! Will the fairy girl change my head into a donkey's head like she did in the play?"

My fists went tight and I jumped to my feet. I kept my temper. "I do not need to change your head into a donkey's. It is ugly enough already." I felt pleased with that.

She raised one red-brown eyebrow. "I could act better than you," she said. "In fact, there's a cat in the back alley that could act better than you! You try to skip around like a girl," she laughed, dancing around the room clumsily. "Dad's chickens can dance better than you."

The landlord appeared in the doorway. "That's enough, Miranda," he said to her.

"Yes, Father," she sighed.

She walked to the door, turned for one last look at me, and stuck out her tongue.

The landlord cleared his throat and called, "His lordship, the Earl of Essex is here to see Master Shakespeare!"

There was a sudden silence in the room, then a great shuffling of chairs as the actors hurried to empty the room.

I stood there with my mouth open as the tall, handsome, and richly dressed earl marched into the room, sword clattering at his side and long beard flowing. He was the old queen's favorite and her most powerful lord.

Some people whispered she wanted to marry him and make him her king! Some whispered she was annoyed because he acted like a king already.

Suddenly, I felt my arm pulled viciously. It was the Miranda girl. She dragged me to the doorway. "It's a secret meeting, half-wit! Get out!"

But I wondered what the secret was.

The Master of the Globe

The earl pulled the curtain across the door. The passage where I stood was dark. I stayed at the curtain and heard the Earl of Essex talk to my master, William Shakespeare.

"William, my friend, how are you?" the earl boomed.

Mr. Shakespeare said, "This is an honor!"

"It's an honor for me," the earl told him.

"That's what I meant—an honor for you!" Mr. Shakespeare laughed, and the earl joined the laughter.

Suddenly the girl hissed in my ear, "Spy!"

"It can't be that secret or they wouldn't be talking so loud," I said.

"Big ears," she sneered at me.

"Donkey ears," I spat back in the dim light.

Suddenly, we knew that the two men were talking quietly now.

We both crept back to the curtain to listen. And what we heard was the thing that almost cost me my life.

"Next Wednesday, you are doing a play at The Globe theater, aren't you, William?" the earl was asking.

"We are doing my play, *The Merchant of Venice*," my master told him.

"Hmm," the Earl of Essex said, and we heard his feet pacing the floor of the room. The girl, Miranda, snatched the knife from my belt. I almost cried out.

The footsteps stopped. Miranda used my knife to make a small slit in the curtain. She handed me back my knife, then put her eye to the hole she had made.

I copied her.

The tall earl was looking out of the window. "I want you to perform your play about King Richard the Second," he said.

Master Shakespeare shook his head slowly. "It's a long time since we did that. Some of my actors have never done it. We need more than a week to get it ready," he argued. "Next month, maybe."

The earl turned. "No, it *must* be next Wednesday." He walked back to the table where my master sat. "You can do it, William."

Master Shakespeare spread his hands. "But the queen hates that play. It is a play about rebels who kill their king. She is terrified that it will give people ideas. She is scared someone will see the play and try to kill her!"

The earl took a purse from his belt and threw it on the table. "There has been a plague all summer. The theaters have been closed. They have just opened again, and you are desperate for money, William."

"Yes, but ..."

"There are 40 shillings in cash in that purse. Your actors can be paid again, and eat and drink in a good tavern—not a rat hole like this place!"

Miranda suddenly went stiff, and I thought she was going to cry out.

But at that moment, the earl marched toward the curtain, and we stood up and tumbled down the dark hallway, out of sight, until the tall man left.

Later that evening, Master Shakespeare called the actors together. "The good news is that you can be paid at last."

The men and boys all cheered.

"The bad news is we must work night and day so we can perform *Richard II* next Wednesday."

So Master Shakespeare had taken the bribe. It was a huge and deadly mistake that would cost a man his head.

The next week was madder than Prince Hamlet's granny. Every morning we were up at dawn to practice *Richard II,* and every afternoon we acted *A Midsummer Night's Dream*—in the middle of winter!

At night, we had dinner at the Black Bull. On Tuesday night, Miranda served my chicken broth without spilling it. She hissed in my ear, "You're getting better, fairy!"

"I have a bigger part in *Richard II,*" I told her.

"I'll have to come and see you tomorrow afternoon," she said and smiled. I decided it would be the best performance of my life. I didn't know it could have been the last performance of my life.

The Globe theater packed in 2,000 people. The flag flew over the theater to show the play was about to start.

I was squinting through the curtains to see if I could see where Miranda was standing. At the back of the theater, in the shadow of the little rooms, men were gathering and talking.

I couldn't take my eyes off them: men in rich cloaks and swords—only a gentleman could wear a sword; men with hard faces, speaking from the corners of tight mouths.

They all moved up to the Earl of Essex, had a few whispered words, and then settled to watch the play. Somehow I knew I was watching a plot being hatched. A plot to put the Earl of Essex on the throne.

A cannon fired and I jumped—but it was only the signal for our play to begin.

The play went well, but when our King Richard was murdered, the gentlemen in the shadows laughed and nodded happily.

When we danced a jig at the end of the play, I leapt higher than anyone. Miranda cheered and clapped. I was happy.

The next day, the rebellion came. It was one day that would go down in history. At the time, it was a shock and a wonder … and I was there!

"Rebellion!" someone cried in the hallway of the Black Bull the next morning. We dragged on our clothes and stumbled to the door, still half asleep.

Two hundred riders clattered down the road toward Westminster Hall. Gentlemen with glittering swords and fine horses—the same gentlemen who had met at the theater the day before. At the head of the riders was the Earl of Essex.

"Join me, my friends," he cried to the people on the streets. "The queen is too old to rule! It is time she went off into some quiet country palace to spend her last days in peace! Let me rule England, my dear friends. Follow me to Richmond Palace. When the queen sees you all, she will know it is time to go!"

An old man and his wife worked in the Black Bull. They looked out at the earl.

"What did he say?" the old woman said, and her voice trembled.

"He says he wants to be queen!" the old man muttered through his toothless mouth.

"He can't do that!" his wife laughed. She stuck her head out into the street. "Here! Young man! You can't be queen! We've already got one!"

Then she ducked back in before he could see who had shouted.

The crowd laughed and shuffled their feet and began to drift away.

The old woman became braver.

"Go home to your mother!" she screeched. "And put that sword away before you cut yourself!" She ducked back in.

The earl was becoming desperate.

"You have had years of plague and years of hunger. You people of England have had to feed your children on cats, and dogs, and even nettle roots!"

"I'll bet it tastes better than my wife's cooking!" the old man called, joining in the fun. His wife smacked him on the head with a wet cloth.

"People of England, I beg you. Join me! Join me! Join me!" the earl roared.

"Why do you need joining?" the old woman screamed. "Are you falling apart?"

Furious horsemen raised their swords and looked toward the Black Bull.

"You'll get yourself chopped," her husband warned her.

"No, she won't," a voice behind him said. "It's the Earl of Essex who'll get himself chopped." It was Master Shakespeare, and he was right.

The queen's troops arrived in an hour, and they met the earl's little band of rebels. The people of London refused to join his revolt. The 200 gentlemen gave up after only a short struggle.

But my struggles were just about to begin.

The Cold, Gray Prison

Once the Earl of Essex had been locked in the Tower of London, the queen sent her soldiers after all the people who may have helped the revolt—people like us.

Master Shakespeare and our acting troupe were dragged from our beds that night and taken to the prison at Newgate.

They gave us water. If we wanted a candle for light, wood for a fire, straw for a bed, or food, then we had to pay. I had no money.

I slept on the cold stone floor and wept. The next day, Miranda brought me some bread and cheese. One of the thieves who shared my cell stole it.

After three days, I was taken before Lord Cecil—the man the queen called her dwarf. As I said, I was almost fainting with fear as I faced the monster queen.

"When you acted out your play, *Richard II*, that was a signal for all the plotters to meet to start the rebellion," Lord Cecil said.

"I know that now," I nodded.

"The question is, did Mr. Shakespeare know that? Was he part of the plot?" Queen Elizabeth asked, and her white makeup cracked around the eyes as she scowled at me.

"Mr. Shakespeare had no idea!" I told her.

She jabbed a claw finger at me. "Mr. Shakespeare had a meeting with the Earl of Essex a week before the play was shown. A secret meeting."

"But the earl didn't tell my master why he wanted to see that play!" I cried.

The queen gave a sour smile. "How would you know?" she hissed. "It was a secret meeting."

"I was listening at the door," I told her.

Lord Cecil looked at me sharply. "Were you? By God's nails, you are the only person who knows the truth then!"

"I do!" I nodded.

The queen snorted. "You would lie to save your precious Master Shakespeare," she said.

"But ..."

"'Don't argue with me," she went on fiercely. "There is only one way to make sure you are telling the truth." She turned to her little minister. "Take him to the Tower. Let the torturers work on him. Screw his thumbs until they bleed and stretch him on the rack until he's six feet tall!"

Lord Cecil bowed low and turned to one of the guards.

"Wait!" I said. "There was someone else there—a girl. It was the innkeeper's daughter. She's not a friend of Master Shakespeare. She'll tell the truth!"

Lord Cecil looked at the queen. After a minute, she said, "Send for her."

It took two hours for the queen's guard to find Miranda and bring her to the palace. Two hours in which I had a hideous thought. I had saved myself from torture for a little while, but maybe they would torture Miranda instead.

The Willing Witness

Miranda came into the queen's great hall, dropped a curtsy, and looked at me with a frown. I didn't dare meet her stare.

Suddenly, Queen Elizabeth rose from the throne and hobbled toward Miranda.

"Don't be afraid, girl," she said, and her voice was suddenly sweet.

"I'm not afraid, your majesty. Just curious," Miranda said pertly.

"Ah! A brave-hearted lass. I like that."

The queen did something I didn't expect. She smiled.

Lord Cecil put questions to Miranda and she answered them quickly. "And do you think Master Shakespeare knew this was part of the plot?"

"Oh, no!" Miranda smiled. "He only did it for the money—40 shillings."

Lord Cecil looked at the queen. "Shall I have the girl tortured now, your majesty?" he asked.

Miranda gasped. "Tortured?" She glared at me, and I knew she'd never forgive me now that she saw the danger I had led her into. "Why?"

But Queen Elizabeth snapped, "Don't be foolish, dwarf! The girl is clearly a truthful child."

Lord Cecil shrugged his shoulders. "I thought the boy was truthful—but you wanted him tortured. How can you tell the girl is not a liar?" he asked.

The queen placed a wrinkled hand on Miranda's head. "Because she is just like I was when I was her age." The queen patted her frizzy, orange wig, then patted Miranda's head. "The girl has red hair—just like me! We red-haired girls are the bravest and the best people in the whole world. Isn't that so, Miranda?"

Miranda grinned. "We know that, your majesty."

I think my mouth must have fallen open with surprise.

The queen ordered Miranda, "Take this boy back to your tavern and look after him, child. Keep him out of trouble—keep him out of my torture rooms!" she cackled.

"I'll try, your majesty," Miranda promised, as I blushed as red as Elizabeth's wig.

"After all," the queen sighed. "He is just a young man—and we know what men are like."

"Hopeless," Miranda said with a shake of her head. She tossed her head at me. "Well, boy? I'd better get you back to the Black Bull and start looking after you!"

I followed her to the door. I stopped a moment. I looked back. The queen and Lord Cecil were laughing.

"What is it, young man?" Queen Elizabeth asked.

"Couldn't I … Wouldn't you …?"

"What?"

"Wouldn't you … rather send me back to prison?" I groaned.

I felt a sharp tug on my sleeve as I was dragged away from a red-haired queen by a red-haired girl.

Afterword: The Essex Rebellion

The Actor, the Rebel, and the Wrinkled Queen is a story based on real people and events in Tudor times in England.

The Earl of Essex was a wild young man, but old Queen Elizabeth was very fond of him. She called him her Wild Horse.

The earl was known as the most popular man in England. As Elizabeth grew old and feeble, he decided to see if he was popular enough to be chosen as the ruler of England.

First, he had to capture Elizabeth. He gathered the 200 plotters together and rode into London on February 8, 1601. He had made a huge mistake. The people of London were poor, and hungry, and unhappy with the queen's rule. But they weren't traitors. They refused to join Essex. He was arrested without much of a fight.

On February 25, he was beheaded.

The play, *Richard II*, was performed as a signal for the rebellion to begin. Queen Elizabeth was furious that William Shakespeare had acted the play at The Globe theater, and she had him arrested with his actors. The question was, Did Shakespeare know the show was part of a plot? Or did he just perform it for the money? In time, the queen released Shakespeare. She seemed to believe he was not to blame.

But was he? What is the truth? What happened when the Earl of Essex met Shakespeare to ask him to perform? We will never know.

Elizabeth did give Shakespeare and the actors a small punishment for their crime. She said they had to perform a play for her, free of charge. Shakespeare agreed. The queen wanted to show she was not afraid of plots. So what play did she make them perform?

Richard II ... of course!

Look for all the

Historical Tales

by best-selling author Terry Deary

The Actor, the Rebel, and the Wrinkled Queen

The Maid, the Witch, and the Cruel Queen

The Prince, the Cook, and the Cunning King

The Thief, the Fool, and the Big Fat King

The Gold in the Grave

The Magic and the Mummy

The Phantom and the Fisherman

The Plot on the Pyramid